Wild Things

Wild Things

BY BETSY DUFFEY

Illustrated by Susanna Natti

A TRUMPET CLUB SPECIAL EDITION

Published by The Trumpet Club, Inc.,
a subsidiary of Bantam Doubleday Dell Publishing Group, Inc.,
1540 Broadway, New York, New York 10036.
"A Trumpet Club Special Edition" with the portrayal of a
trumpet and two circles is a registered trademark of
Bantam Doubleday Dell Publishing Group, Inc.

ISBN 0-440-83237-3

This edition published by arrangement with Viking Penguin,
a division of Penguin Books USA Inc.

Printed in the United States of America
April 1995
1 3 5 7 9 10 8 6 4 2
OPM

To Alex and Kristin

Contents

Stakeout

Shhh!" said Evie.

"When will they come?" whispered Megan. "My legs are starting to cramp."

"Shhh," said Evie again.

Evie and Megan crouched low behind the trash cans in Evie's backyard. Evie's dog Flea lay beside them asleep. He slept on his back with his legs sprawled out.

It was dark. The girls kept their flashlights turned off and waited.

"I'm cold," Megan said. She shifted and bumped against a metal trash can. It clanged.

Flea looked up and whined.

"Shhh!" said Evie. "They'll hear us." She reached down and patted Flea. He had been one of the first animals the Pet Patrol had helped. When Evie and Megan started the club, their first job had been to find homes for four puppies—Flea and his sister and two brothers.

Flea closed his eyes again. Evie shivered. The summer days were hot but the summer nights were cool. The girls had been hiding behind the trash cans for almost an hour. Where were those boys?

Every night for three nights now someone had been raiding Evie's trash cans. Every morning for three mornings Evie had had to pick up trash in the backyard.

She was tired of the scattered paper, vegetable cans, bread wrappers, and messy coffee grounds. She was tired of spending her waking hours picking up garbage.

The first morning that it happened she hadn't minded so much. It was sort of funny to see the trash scattered everywhere.

It was like the time last Halloween when Matt Morrison and Joe Bates TP'ed the oak tree in the front yard.

Matt and Joe had sold Halloween insurance the day before at school. If you bought the "insurance" for twenty-five cents then they would come and clean up your yard if anything happened to it Halloween night.

Everyone knew that Matt and Joe were the ones

who made things "happen" to yards. Everyone had paid the quarter. Almost.

"You better pay them," Megan had warned Evie.

"No way," Evie said loud enough for Matt and Joe to hear. "That's blackmail."

They saw Matt and Joe whispering later.

"You're going to be sorry," Megan said.

Megan spent Halloween night at Evie's and they sat in front of the picture window hidden by the draperies until past midnight waiting for the boys. They fell asleep in front of the window.

The next morning when Evie and Megan woke up, they looked out and saw the old oak in the front yard covered in toilet paper. Long loops of white draped down like the trimming on a Christmas tree.

Evie and Megan ran outside. Evie's father was staring up at the toilet-paper-covered branches.

"How did it get up there?" Megan asked.

"Well," Evie's father explained, "someone threw a roll of toilet paper high up into the tree. It unrolled in the air and caught on the branches."

"How do we get it down?" Evie asked her father.

"We don't," he said. "First rain will take it right out."

Evie wondered how he knew so much about toilet paper in trees.

Nobody asked who did it.

They all knew it was Matt and Joe.

So, when Evie saw the trash spread out over the backyard her first thought was: Matt and Joe.

Her second thought was: Stakeout.

Evie checked her watch. 9:35.

"Evie?" Megan whispered.

"Shhhh!"

"But, Evie."

"Shhh!"

"But, Evie."

"What?" Evie whispered.

"Here they come!"

Caught in the Act!

Come on!" Evie whispered.

Pong pong pong.

They could hear the sound of a basketball pounding on the street in front of the house. Matt never went anywhere without his basketball.

Pong pong pong.

Flea growled.

"Shh, Flea."

The girls crept silently along the side of the house. Evie held Flea's collar.

Pong pong pong.

The noises were closer now. It sounded as if they were right in front of Evie's house. The girls moved slowly toward the edge of the wall.

"I'm scared," said Megan. "Let's go back into the house. What if it's not Matt and Joe? What if it's a burglar?"

Evie didn't stop. "Burglars don't bounce basket-balls."

They got to the corner and peered around it.

They could see Matt and Joe walking down the street. Matt bounced the ball with each step.

"Let's follow them," said Evie. "We can catch them in the act."

She remembered the trash scattered across the yard and gritted her teeth. They would wait until the boys took the tops off the trash cans. Until they were just reaching in. Then she would say, "*Ah ha!* Caught in the act!"

Grrr.

"Shh, Flea," she whispered. Matt and Joe would not try anything tonight if they heard Flea.

Megan rubbed her arms. "We really shouldn't be doing this, Evie. My mom wouldn't like me to be walking around at night."

"Don't be silly," said Evie. "We're just going down the street. Matt and Joe will double back to my yard any minute."

"Why don't we just wait for them here?"

Evie frowned. "I want to see what else they do. I'm going." She stepped out of the shadow of the house.

"If you want to wait here . . . in the dark . . . by yourself . . ."

"I'm coming," said Megan quickly.

She looked back and forth at the dark bushes, then followed Evie down the sidewalk.

Everything looked different at night. The street-lights cast shadows on the pavement. Evie and Megan stayed in the shadows and followed the *pong pong pong* of the basketball.

Flea pulled at his leash. He wanted to get to the boys. Up ahead Evie could see the glow of flashlights.

"They did it," she whispered to Megan. "I know they did."

"How can you be sure?"

"They're always up to something. You know they were the ones who put the whoopee cushion on my chair during my book report last year. Right?"

"Right."

"And we know they were the ones who put your gym suit up the flagpole. Right?"

"Right."

"And don't forget the toilet paper in my oak tree last Halloween. They are *wild*. Everyone in Mrs. Roper's class last year called them the Wild Things."

Megan giggled.

"Shhh."

Pong pong pong.

The sounds were just ahead but they couldn't see Matt and Joe anymore.

"They're not doubling back," said Megan. "We're going too far. Let's go back."

"Just one more block," said Evie.

"Grrr," said Flea.

Up ahead the basketball stopped bouncing.

Evie held up her hand to signal Megan to stop. They moved closer into the shadow of some bushes. There was no sound now.

Flea whined and turned to face the bushes. Evie tried to pull him back but he turned again.

"Where are they?" Megan whispered. "I don't like this. I . . ."

Evie frowned. She didn't like it, either. Flea growled at the bushes again.

"Let's go home. Let's . . ."

Suddenly, loud noises came from the bushes beside them. Noises of someone or something crashing through the brush. Through the brush toward them.

Flea's hair stood on end. He let out one loud bark. Megan screamed. Evie stood frozen.

The bushes parted. Evie pointed her flashlight into the bushes—right into the faces of Matt and Joe.

Matt pointed a finger accusingly at the girls.

"Ah ha!" he said. *"Caught in the act!"*

Did Not!

Run for it!" Evie yelled.

She ran back down Carter's Mill Road. Flea ran along beside her, barking and wagging his tail. He pulled on his leash.

"Come on, Flea!" Evie called.

Flea twisted his neck and popped out of his collar. He bounded ahead, his ears flapping in the wind.

Evie could hear Megan breathing hard beside her. Their feet pounded the pavement toward home. Behind them they heard the pounding feet of Matt and Joe. They had to escape the Wild Things.

Behind them Matt let out a war whoop.

The girls sped up.

They ran past Mr. Shivers's house. Matt and Joe followed.

They ran past Mrs. Hansen's house. Matt and Joe followed.

Finally they reached the edge of Evie's yard. They cut across the damp grass and ran up the stairs to the porch. Flea disappeared around the side of the house.

They collapsed exhausted on the porch. At least they felt safe here.

Then Evie stood up. It was time to face the boys. She pushed a loose strand of hair out of her face and put her hands on her hips. She tried to catch her breath.

Matt and Joe crossed the last few feet of grass and stopped at the bottom of the steps.

They looked up at Evie. They were out of breath, too.

Now she would make them admit what they had done.

Megan stood behind her.

"You," she said, pointing to the boys, "have been dumping out my trash and I know it!"

Matt and Joe looked surprised. "Wait a minute," said Matt. "We caught *you*. You've been dumping out *my* trash! Don't try to get out of it by accusing us."

Beside him, Joe nodded.

Evie's mouth tightened. "I," she said, "am not the one trying to get out of it! *You* were the ones who put toilet paper in my oak tree last Halloween."

She watched their expressions.

Joe giggled. Matt looked at him and tried not to grin. Evie saw the look.

"It *was* you," she said. "And you were the ones who put the whoopee cushion on my chair during my book report last year."

Joe giggled again.

"It *was* you!" Evie said again. "And Megan's gym suit?"

Matt held up his hands. "Okay," he said. "*That* was us. But the trash dumping is *you*."

Evie stamped her foot. "Don't try to get out of it. You did it."

"Did not!"

"Did too!"

"Did not!"

"Did—"

From behind the house came the clank of a trash-can lid. From behind the house came the barks of an excited dog.

Without a word Evie and Megan and Matt and Joe ran toward the sounds. They ran around the corner of the house and stopped.

They turned their flashlights to the yard. In the beams of light they saw scattered paper, vegetable cans, bread wrappers, and coffee grounds. The yard was covered with trash.

The cans were turned on their sides, empty.

Flea stood in the middle of the mess, barking. The hair on his back stood on end.

"Flea!" Evie yelled.

He stopped barking and walked toward Evie. He wagged his tail as he walked.

Evie turned to Matt. "It wasn't you," she said. She shook her head. "We've been watching you all night."

Megan looked puzzled. "If it wasn't you, who was it?"

Flea lay down beside Evie and rested his head on her foot.

Joe looked at Matt and Evie and Megan.

"Looks like we know now who it was," he said.

"Who?" said Evie.

Joe pointed his finger at Flea and gave Evie a serious look. "There!" he said. "There is the criminal." Flea rolled his eyes up at Matt and Joe. He thumped his tail.

"No!" Evie said.

"There's the proof," said Matt, waving his arm at the backyard. "We caught him in the act!"

"You didn't *see* him do it," said Evie.

"Well, I heard him," said Matt.

Joe nodded. Megan kneeled and put her arm around Flea.

"Flea would never do anything like that," she said.

"Okay," said Matt. "How do you explain this?" He pointed to the trash strewn across the yard. "And," he continued, "he must be the one who's raiding my trash cans, too."

Evie frowned. "I don't know who or what did it," she said. "But I do know that it wasn't Flea. He's innocent! Some other animal must have come out of the woods to do it. Flea chased them off. That's why he was barking. He's not guilty. He's a hero!"

Matt laughed. "A *hero?* He's a criminal."

"Hero!" said Evie.

"Criminal!"

"Hero!"

"Criminal!"

"Prove it!" Evie said.

Matt was silent for a moment. "Okay," he said. "I'll prove it."

"You can never prove it," said Evie.

"Never?" Matt smiled. "If I can prove it and I'm right then what do I get?"

"Name it!" said Evie.

"Let's see." He turned to Joe. They whispered together for a moment, then turned back to Evie and Megan.

"If we can prove it, then we get to be members of the Pet Patrol."

Evie and Megan gasped at the same time. "You?" Evie said. "In our club?"

"Yes," Matt said. "And if we can't prove it then you get something."

"What do we get?" asked Megan.

"You name it," said Matt.

Evie turned to Megan. It only took one second. She turned back to Matt and Joe.

"If you're wrong, then no more pranks on me or Megan."

"Never?"

"Never."

Matt and Joe whispered again. They turned back to the girls.

"Deal," said Matt.

"Deal," said Evie.

"Get ready to make us members."

"Get ready to stop all your pranks."

"Just wait," said Matt. "We'll have all the evidence we need in the morning!"

Pong pong pong.

Matt began to bounce the basketball. The boys headed back down the street.

Megan looked at Evie. Evie looked back at Megan.

Megan slowly shook her head and said, "What have we done?"

Hot Dogs!

Evie watched the boys leave. The glow of their flashlights faded as they walked down the street.

Pong pong pong.

The sound of the basketball echoed in the night air and became fainter and fainter. Megan looked at Evie.

"Evie," she said, "I can't believe that you said we would let Matt and Joe be members of the Pet Patrol! We've always been serious about our club. We want to help a lot of animals and do a lot of good things. If Matt and Joe join they won't be serious. They'll make everything into a joke." Megan sighed.

"Like cheerleading tryouts," she continued. "Remember that time they got behind Marge Gabel at cheerleading tryouts and imitated her?"

Evie tried not to smile. She thought about Matt and Joe standing in the background with pom-poms doing the cheers behind Marge.

"Tryouts were ruined," Megan said. "And remember the Valentine's Day party when they put fake valentines into everyone's bags?"

Evie swallowed a giggle. "Mine said, 'I love you meet me after school,' and it was signed 'Travis Martin.' "

Megan smiled. "Mine said, 'I want to go steady with you.' It was signed 'Spence Rattray.' "

"Remember Tiffie thought hers was real . . ."

They both giggled.

Then Evie looked serious. "The Valentine's Day party was ruined. We can't let that happen to the Pet Patrol. They'll be wild. The Pet Patrol will be finished."

"The Pet Patrol will not be finished," said Evie. "Because Flea didn't do it."

Megan looked doubtful. "Can you be sure?" she asked.

Evie looked up in surprise. "Megan, not you too! You don't think he did it, do you?"

"Well . . ."

"Megan!"

"How can you be sure, Evie?"

"I know Flea," said Evie. "Besides, I think I know now who is doing it."

"Who?" said Megan.

"Well, there are woods behind my house. The trash cans are back by the woods. Flea ran back and began barking. Did you see how the hair was standing up on his back?"

Megan nodded. She reached down and gave Flea a few reassuring pats.

"He only does that when there's another animal around. He scared off the animal, Megan."

"What kind of animal do you think it is?" Megan asked.

"I don't know that," said Evie. "But I do know that whatever kind of animal it is, it needs help."

"Why?"

"Because it's hungry. It's raiding trash cans for food. This is an animal with a problem."

Megan nodded. "Sounds like a job for . . ."

"The Pet Patrol!" they said together.

Evie looked at Megan with determination. "We need to figure out what kind of animal it is. Then we can decide how to help that animal."

Megan nodded. "Let's start first thing in the morning."

"Come on," Evie said. "We need to do one more thing tonight."

Megan frowned. "It really is late, Evie. Your parents will start to worry."

"Matt and Joe are going to do something tonight. Let's go see what they're up to before we go in. It will just take five minutes."

"I don't know," Megan said.

"They said they'd have some evidence in the morning, so they must be planning something. And knowing Matt and Joe, it will probably be some kind of trick."

Megan nodded. "You're right. I guess we better check it out."

Evie and Megan walked down the street. They circled Matt's house and crept up behind his backyard. They could see the boys in the floodlights behind the house.

"What are they doing?" said Megan.

"I don't know," said Evie.

Matt and Joe were working in the backyard. Joe was digging in the dirt around the trash cans. Matt was raking the dirt and smoothing it out.

"I think I know," said Megan. "It must be a track pit."

"What's a track pit?"

"Look," Megan explained. "Joe is loosening up the

dirt around the cans. Matt is raking it to smooth it out. Whatever is raiding the trash cans will leave its prints in the dirt."

Evie nodded. "I think you're right," she said. "Then they can tell by the shape of the print whether it's a skunk or a cat, or a porcupine or a possum . . ."

"Or a dog," Megan said.

"It is *not* a dog," said Evie.

"Shh, they'll hear us."

Matt went into the house. Joe leaned on the shovel and waited.

"Let's go home," said Megan. "Now we know the plan. And it's perfect, Evie. They really will find out what kind of animal it is. They'll prove that Flea is innocent."

"One more minute," said Evie. "Let's just see what Matt is going in the house to get."

Matt came back out, carrying a small package. He opened it.

"What is it? I can't see," said Evie. "He's tying something to the lid of the trash can."

The girls moved closer.

They could hear Matt laughing with Joe as he tied one thing after another to the top of the trash-can lids.

Flea whined and pulled forward on his leash.

"Hot dogs!" said Evie.

"Hot dogs?" said Megan.

"They're tying hot dogs to the lid. Flea loves hot dogs, and Matt knows it! When Flea and I did the talent show at school, I used hot dogs for his rewards. Flea will do anything for a bite of hot dog!"

Flea sniffed the air, then pulled forward and tried to twist his neck out of the collar.

"Cheaters!" whispered Megan. "This is hopeless."

"Flea has already smelled the hot dogs," said Evie. "First chance he gets he'll go right to the trash cans."

"We're sunk."

"Maybe we're not sunk yet," said Evie. "We'll take Flea home and lock him up. In the morning they'll know the truth. The real trash-can raider will come and leave his prints. And it won't be Flea."

Flea strained on his leash as they pulled him forward, away from Matt's house and the hot dogs.

"The important thing tonight," said Evie, "is to be sure that Flea does not get out of the house."

She gave Flea one more tug and they headed for home.

"In the morning the mystery will be solved!"

No Hot Dogs

Evie woke up and stretched. Megan was still sleeping in the other twin bed in her room.

"*E*-vie! *Me*-gan!" A voice called from outside.

Pong pong pong.

"*E*-vie! *Me*-gan!" It was a taunting voice. It was the voice of Matt.

"Megan!" Evie said. "It's Matt and Joe outside! Wake up!" She threw a stuffed teddy bear at Megan.

Megan did not move.

"Wake *up!*" Evie said again. She looked around her room.

Where was Flea?

"Flea!" she called out.

No answer.

She looked under the bed where he liked to sleep. No Flea.

"Megan, Flea's gone!" She threw a spotted giraffe. Megan finally sat up and rubbed her eyes.

"What?" she said.

"Flea's gone!" Evie looked at the door of her room. It was open.

"Evie! Megan!" The voice called again.

Pong pong pong.

"Oh, no," Evie groaned. She pulled on a pair of shorts and grabbed a T-shirt. "Let's go!" she said.

Megan got up and began to get dressed.

"They must have the proof," Megan said. "I knew this would happen. I told you, Evie. I . . ."

"Come on."

They ran downstairs.

"Evie!" her mother called from the kitchen. "You girls want some breakfast?"

"In a minute, Mom," Evie called. Then she stopped by the kitchen door. "Mom, did you let Flea out of my room last night?"

"Yes," her mother answered. "He was whining so pitifully at the door to your room that I just had to let him out."

Evie looked at Megan. "We'll be right back, Mom," she said. They headed out the front door.

"Hello, fellow Pet Patrol members!" Matt called from the sidewalk. "Come and see the evidence!"

Joe held up a white sheet of paper. "Guilty!" he said.

Flea sat beside Matt and thumped his tail.

Joe handed Evie the white paper. On it Joe had drawn a footprint. The footprint had a triangular palm with four oval fingers, and at the top of each finger was a nail print.

"Look," said Matt. He rested his basketball on his hip and pulled a small nature book out of his pocket. He turned to a page where he had put a bookmark.

"Here's the proof."

On the next few pages were animal footprints. One for each kind of animal. Each was labeled with an animal's name.

There was a two-inch print, shaped like a hand with four fingers. It was labeled Squirrel.

There was a six-inch print that had webs between the toes like a duck. It was labeled Beaver.

There was one that looked like a small star-shaped hand, two inches long. It was labeled Possum.

There was one labeled Deer, one labeled Raccoon, and one labeled Dog.

Evie looked at the paper drawing, then at the book. The drawing matched the print marked Dog.

"We copied this from the dirt around my trash cans! You can go and look for yourself if you don't believe us. There are plenty more prints like this over there. Now what do you say?"

"I say that doesn't prove anything," said Evie. "That could have been *any* dog, not *my* dog."

"Let's compare the print to Flea's foot," said Joe. "Let's see if it matches."

Evie hesitated.

"Unless you're afraid," said Matt.

Evie frowned at Matt and gave a whistle. Flea came running. "Sit, Flea," she said.

He sat.

"Shake hands, Flea," she said and Flea held up one paw.

Joe took the paw and looked at it. He held the paper up to the paw.

"Ah ha!" he said. "Looks like we have a match."

The prints were the same size.

"Aren't you going to welcome us to the Pet Patrol?"

"Not so fast," said Megan. "There's still some doubt here."

"Not in my mind," said Matt. "How much more

proof can you have? Here's a print. It's a dog print.
It matches your dog."

"It matches," said Megan, "because you put hot
dogs on your trash can last night!"

"You spied on us!"

"Yes!" said Evie, "and it's a good thing we did.
The only thing you've proved is that dogs like hot
dogs. Not that *this* dog was raiding your trash cans."

Matt frowned.

"You can't deny it!" said Evie.

"Well," said Matt. "Uh . . . we just thought a little
bait would . . ."

Evie tapped her foot.

Matt looked at Joe. Joe stepped forward.

"Maybe the hot dogs weren't a good idea," he said.

"Maybe not," said Megan.

"What would be enough proof? What if I had a
way to catch him in the act and could prove it?"

"No hot dogs?" Megan said.

"No hot dogs," Matt agreed.

"If you could catch him in the act without using
hot dogs," said Evie, "that would be enough."

"Okay," said Matt. "Tonight we'll catch him in
the act! Come on, Joe. We have work to do."

They headed back down the street.

"They're serious," said Megan. "They're making plans."

Evie stared at the paper in her hand.

"You're right," she said. "We have to be careful."

She looked down at Flea.

"It's time to make some plans of our own."

Kodak Moments

Evie sat on the front steps of her house. Megan sat beside her. Evie's mother brought out two blueberry muffins and two glasses of orange juice on a bamboo tray.

"Here you go, girls," she said, putting down the tray.

Neither girl moved.

"What's up?" Evie's mother asked.

"Pet Patrol case," Evie answered. "We're trying to solve the mystery of the trash cans."

"Some animal is raiding the trash," Megan added.

"I know," said Evie's mother. "And it's becoming a nuisance. I think the Murphys must have been feeding a wild animal behind their house."

"But they moved last week," said Megan.

"Right," Evie's mother said. "When they moved out, the animal lost his food supply."

"Hmmm." Evie nodded. "He got used to eating handouts. Now he's looking for food at our houses."

"We have to help that animal," said Megan.

Evie's mother looked serious. "Now, you girls be careful. Wild things can carry diseases. They are not pets. They can be dangerous."

"We know," said Evie. She giggled. "Especially the two Wild Things that live down the street!" Her mother smiled as she walked back inside.

Evie picked up one of the hot muffins. "We need a plan," she said to Megan.

Flea lay down on the bottom step and rested his head between his paws. He looked up at Evie. He thumped his tail. He got into begging position.

Evie reached down and gave him a piece of her muffin.

"You're right, Evie," Megan said. She took a sip of orange juice. "We need our own plan. We can't just wait for Matt and Joe to solve this mystery. We need to do it ourselves."

"Should we have another stakeout?" Evie asked.

"I don't think another stakeout will work."

Evie nodded. "Last night the animal didn't come until after we left. We probably scared it off."

They thought for a moment.

Megan looked at Evie. "We need a way to see the trash cans at night without being there."

Evie looked up. "How about a camera?"

"Hmmm . . ." said Megan slowly. "If we aren't there, how can we take the picture? And it'll be too dark . . ."

They thought again.

"My dad has an old flash camera. Remember the one I always use?" Evie said. "It can take a picture in the dark. If we could only find a way for the camera to take a picture at the right time without us . . ."

"Like a trip wire," said Megan.

"What's a trip wire?"

"A trip wire is a piece of string stretched across the path where an animal walks. He steps on it and it triggers something. Like a trap, or in this case, a camera."

"Cool!" said Evie. "My dad has lots of books about cameras. Maybe one will show us how to do it."

"Let's try it," said Megan.

They took their dishes back to the kitchen. Evie ran upstairs and got the camera. The girls sat on the floor in the living room by the bookcase. Evie pulled down the camera books one at a time and looked through the tables of contents.

"No," she said after the first book.

"No," after the second.

She pulled out the third book.

"Yes!" she said. "Here's a chapter called 'Camera Traps.' " She flipped through the book to the right page.

"How does it work?" Megan said, leaning over Evie's shoulder to look at the book.

"It says we need a camera that has a lever on the side instead of a button on the top."

"Oh, no—"

"This *has* a lever!" said Evie, holding up the camera.

"Good," said Megan. "What else do we need?"

The girls gathered the things quickly. A mousetrap, string, a stake, a nail, a hammer.

They carried everything to the backyard and began to set up their camera trap.

First Evie attached the camera to the top of a fence post. She focused it on the trash cans.

Then Megan tied the string to the lever on the camera. "Be careful," said Evie. "If you pull that string, it will take a picture."

Click!

"Oops," said Megan. "I took my own picture. It's a Kodak Moment!" She giggled.

"Be serious," said Evie. She nailed the mousetrap to the bottom of the post and tied the string from the camera to the little bar on the trap.

"Look," she said. "When the mousetrap snaps shut, it will pull the string and the camera will . . ."

Click!

"Oops," said Megan. "You got yourself!"

"Another Kodak Moment?" Evie said.

Both girls giggled.

"What makes the mousetrap snap?" Megan asked.

"That's where your trip wire comes in," said Evie. She pounded the stake into the ground beside the trash cans. She ran another piece of string from the stake across to the fence post and attached it to the trigger of the mousetrap.

"Okay, let's try it," she said. "You are the animal, Megan. Now walk toward the trash cans."

Megan walked toward the cans.

As her foot stepped on the trip wire, she smiled at the camera and put her hand behind her head like a movie star. The mousetrap snapped.

Click!

"Perfect!" said Evie.

"It worked!" said Megan. "Try it, Evie."

They set the mousetrap again. They wound the film.

"Ready?" said Evie. She jumped forward onto the string on one foot in a ballet pose. "Taa Daa!" she said.

Click!

Both girls giggled again.

"Well, the trip wire works," Evie said. "Now we just have to hope that the animal comes this way and that it steps on the string."

"I know it will," said Megan.

"Great," said Evie. "Our plan is ready!"

Megan smiled. "Now it's time to see what the Wild Things are planning!"

Doggy Yummies

We need spy equipment," Evie said. "Let's see what we can find in my room." They hurried upstairs.

"How about those binoculars?" said Megan, pointing to Evie's shelf.

"Perfect!" Evie picked up the binoculars and put the strap around her neck.

"What else do we need?" said Megan.

"I don't know," said Evie. "How about hats?"

"What do hats have to do with spying?"

"Disguises," answered Evie.

They looked at Evie's hat collection. There was a white Styrofoam hat with a red-white-and-blue ribbon around it, a railroad cap, a straw beach hat, five baseball caps from different teams, and a black top hat.

Evie chose a blue baseball cap. She tucked her hair up inside it. She found a pair of sunglasses and put them on.

Megan looked over the hats. She chose the black top hat. "I'll go in style," she giggled.

"How about Flea?"

Evie looked down at Flea. "He stays home," she said. "He's caused enough trouble." Flea whined as the girls slipped out of the room and closed the door.

They walked down toward Matt's house, staying close to the bushes at the side of the road. When they got near the house they circled Matt's yard and came up behind the hedge again. Evie peeked through it.

"What are they up to now?" said Megan.

"Matt's father is with them," said Evie. "They're taking something out of his van."

"Let me have a look," said Megan. She took the binoculars and looked through the hedge at Mr. Morrison and the boys.

"It's some kind of crate," she said. "A crate with wire on the sides. A crate with a hinged door."

"A *trap!*"

"Yes," said Megan, "a trap."

She put the binoculars down and looked straight at Evie. "They're going to try to catch Flea," she said.

"Mr. Morrison wouldn't be trying to catch Flea," said Evie. "A trap isn't a bad idea. He probably got the trap from the Nature Center."

Megan nodded. They watched Mr. Morrison put the trap in the backyard. He talked to Matt and Joe for a moment, then went inside.

"Matt and Joe are setting the trap now," said Megan, watching through the binoculars.

"Look! They're bringing out the bait," she said. "They're laughing."

"What is it?"

Megan focused the binoculars on the boys. "It's some kind of box."

She squinted into the binoculars. "I can almost make out the writing on the box," she said.

She let the binoculars dangle around her neck and turned to give Evie her most serious look. "The box says 'Doggy Yummies'!"

"Cheaters!" Evie yelled. She ran out from the bushes. Megan followed close behind her.

Matt held the box behind his back. "What are you talking about?" he asked innocently.

"I'm talking about that box of Doggy Yummies behind your back!"

"Oh," said Matt.

"What were you going to do with them, Matt?" asked Megan. "You don't even have a dog."

"I was going to . . . er . . . I was going to . . ."

"Yes, Matt? Does your dad know what you're using for bait?"

Matt turned red. "I was going to give them to you, Evie . . . for Flea."

He held the box out to Evie. "Yes, that's what I was going to do. Just to . . . uh . . . to say we're sorry about the hot dogs." He smiled at Evie.

"You weren't going to use them as bait?"

Matt looked hurt. "Would we do something under-handed like that?" he said.

"Yes!" said Evie and Megan together.

"The idea is to try to find out what animal is doing this—not to frame an innocent dog!" said Evie.

Evie took the box of treats. "No more underhanded pranks!" she said. "Let's go, Megan. Good-bye, cheaters!"

Evie and Megan turned toward the street.

"Oh, E-vie, Me-gan," Matt called in a teasing voice.

"Now what?" said Evie.

Matt giggled and punched Joe with his elbow. "Nice hats," he said.

The giggle turned into a laugh. Joe joined in and they both fell to the ground rolling and laughing.

"Our disguises!" said Evie. She reached up and pulled off the baseball cap and glasses.

"We forgot!" said Megan.

She snatched off her top hat. They ran for the street. They ran all the way back to Evie's house and flopped on the porch out of breath.

"I don't trust them one bit!" Megan said. "We need to keep Flea inside tonight."

"Let's see if you can spend the night again," said Evie. "Will your mom let you?"

"Yes," Megan said. "It's summer."

"Those cheaters," Evie said. "Just wait until morning. We'll show them!"

The Proof

Flea whined and scratched at Evie's bedroom door. He wanted out.

"No, Flea," said Evie.

They were getting ready for bed. "You can't go out," Evie said. When Flea heard the word *out* he barked.

"No, Flea."

Megan attached his leash to his collar, then tied it to Evie's bedpost. They closed Evie's bedroom door. As a last measure Evie tied a jingle bell to Flea's collar. If he got up in the middle of the night they would hear the bell and wake up.

"Well," said Evie, "I think we're safe." Flea lay down beside the bed and put his head on his paws.

Megan agreed. "There's no way he can get out this time."

Evie turned out the light and they went to sleep.

Evie woke up three times in the middle of the night. Each time she reached down beside her bed and felt around for Flea. When her hand touched his soft back she closed her eyes and went back to sleep.

Morning came. Evie woke up. She stretched. She rolled over and closed her eyes for a few more minutes of sleep. She put her hand down to pat Flea. Her hand reached to the right, then to the left.

No Flea.

Evie hung over the bed and peered underneath.

She groaned.

There was the empty collar. There was the bell, chewed off of the collar. The door was open. Flea was gone.

"Where's Flea?"

Evie and Megan ran downstairs into the kitchen. Evie's father looked up from the newspaper in surprise. "Why, he was scratching to get out of your room in the middle of the night, so I let him out."

Evie groaned. Megan groaned.

Evie looked at Megan. "If I know Flea, he remembered the hot dogs and headed right to Matt's."

Megan frowned. "If he did then it's too late to stop him now."

Evie nodded, then looked up at Megan. "The

camera!" she said. They ran into the backyard and looked at the camera. The mousetrap had snapped.

"We got it!" said Evie. "It took a picture!"

"Great!" said Megan. Then she frowned. "You don't think that Flea might have . . ."

"No!" said Evie. "He would never bother the trash. The animal that has been raiding the trash cans is the one on the film! We just need to get the film developed."

Megan took the camera off of the post, rewound the film, and took it out. "The Fast Photo Shop opens at ten o'clock," she said. "If we drop it off at ten it will be ready at eleven."

She handed Evie the film. Evie put it in her pocket. "Okay," she said. "It's time to find Flea."

Evie and Megan ran down the street to Matt's house. They came through the hedge and headed for the trap.

Evie could see that the door of the trap was closed. She could see that something had been caught.

She ran across the backyard to see what it was.

If only it was not Flea! It could be a wild animal— a possum, or a raccoon, or a . . .

Yip!

Flea!

"A-hmm!"

Matt and Joe stood leaning against the back door.

"Looks like we caught ourselves a criminal," Matt said.

"You haven't proven anything," said Evie.

"What do you mean?" said Matt. "We caught him. That *is* the proof. What else would he be doing in my yard at night close to my trash cans? You can't deny it this time, Evie."

Evie frowned at Matt. Then she frowned at Flea in the trap.

"Yip!" Flea barked again. He began to scratch at the side of the cage.

"Go ahead," said Matt. "Take your criminal."

"That's not proof," said Evie.

"Admit it, Evie," said Matt. "This time we got the real evidence, not just a footprint. There"—he pointed at Flea—"is the real proof."

"No, *we* have the real proof," said Evie.

"What are you talking about?" said Joe.

"We set up a camera last night and it took a picture of the animal raiding my trash." She held up the roll of film. "This is the evidence, the true evidence." She waved the film back and forth like a victory trophy.

"How did you do it?" asked Matt.

"We learned how to set up the camera from a book," Evie answered.

"We used a trip wire," Megan added. "When the animal stepped on the trip wire it triggered the camera."

"That's pretty neat," Joe said.

"So," said Evie, "whatever the film shows is the truth, agreed?"

"What if it shows your dog?" said Joe.

Evie's mouth formed a tight line. "It won't," she said.

"But if it does," said Joe, "then *we* win. Agreed?"

"Agreed," said Evie. "But if it shows another animal, then *we* win. Agreed?"

"Agreed," said Joe.

Evie kneeled beside the trap and opened the door. Flea backed out. He gave one happy bark and wiggled back and forth on the grass.

"We'll meet at the Fast Photo Shop at eleven o'clock," said Evie. "The film will be developed, and then we'll know the truth!"

The Real Proof

Evie and Megan pedaled toward the Fast Photo Shop. It was almost eleven o'clock. Flea ran along behind them. The girls didn't talk to each other. Evie thought only of the film. She would show Matt and Joe once and for all.

As they passed Mrs. Hansen's house two small dogs trotted out from her front yard and ran along with Evie and Megan and Flea. They barked at the bikes and wagged their tails. Evie called out to them, "Go home, Waldo. Go home, Ginger!" She watched them turn back and remembered them as tiny puppies. The Pet Patrol had found homes for them then.

They passed the Lewises' house. A small spotted dog lived there. Another dog that the Pet Patrol had helped.

They rounded the corner of Carter's Mill Road and headed toward town. They passed the first and only stoplight in town. Almost there.

The Pet Patrol was about to solve an important case. And the Pet Patrol would *not* be adding two new members!

They pedaled the last few yards to the Fast Photo Shop and parked their bikes. Matt and Joe were already sitting on the curb outside the store.

"Five more minutes," said Joe. He grinned at Evie and Megan.

"Five more minutes," said Matt, "and we will be in your club." He grinned at the girls, too.

"Five more minutes," said Evie, "and we will be rid of your pranks forever."

"Five more minutes," said Megan, "and we will have the real proof."

The girls sat down beside the boys and waited. They could see the man in the store working at a large white machine.

Evie patted Flea. "Good dog," she said.

"Ha!" said Matt.

"He *is* a good dog."

"We'll see."

A voice called from the store. "Hey kids, your pictures are ready!"

Evie jumped up and ran inside. Megan, Matt, and Joe followed.

Evie paid the man. He handed her the envelope of pictures.

"Come on!"

"Open 'em!"

"Let's see!"

The kids jostled the envelope as they walked back out of the shop. Evie opened the flap and pulled out the pile of pictures.

The roll started with Evie and Megan sitting in front of a Christmas tree.

"How old is this film, anyway?" asked Joe.

"Never mind," said Evie.

She flipped through spring and Easter pictures.

Then came a picture of Megan's eye opened wide.

"Cute," Joe said.

Megan snatched the picture away.

Next was Evie's picture when she accidentally triggered the camera. It was a blur.

"Who's that?" said Joe.

"Never mind," said Evie.

Then Megan's picture in the movie-star pose.

Matt snickered. Megan grabbed it.

Then Evie in the ballet pose. Evie shuffled it quickly to the back of the pile.

"I thought we were going to see an animal," said Matt. "Where's this proof?"

Evie flipped to the last picture and stopped.

The four kids stared.

"No!" said Evie.

Matt grabbed the picture and held it high. He held the other hand up, too. He jumped up and down.

"Guilty!" he said.

Joe jumped up with him. "You!" he said, pointing to Flea. "Are guilty!" Flea wagged his tail.

Evie snatched the picture back. She looked at the picture again. Megan leaned over her shoulder.

There was the proof.

In the picture they could see the trash can. It was lying on its side. There in the middle of the picture was Flea. His back paws stood on the string. His front paws were on the side of the overturned trash can.

His eyes glowed white in the flash of the camera. His hair stood on end.

"Flea!" said Evie. "You didn't!"

"He did," said Matt.

"He wouldn't," said Evie.

"He would," said Joe.

Matt clapped hands in a high five with Joe.

"He would and he did," said Matt.

Evie sat down on the curb and she didn't look up. She had lost. Worse than that, Flea had let her down.

"Flea," she said, "did you really do it?"

"Yes!" said Matt. He headed down the street. "Be at my house in ten minutes," he said as he left.

"Yeah," said Joe, "for our first meeting."

"And to hear our plans for the club!"

Megan sat down beside Evie. For a moment they didn't speak. They just stared at the picture.

"We tried," said Megan.

"Yes," said Evie, "we tried. But . . ."

They both stared at the picture again.

"There it is," said Megan, "the real proof."

Evie looked hard at the picture. For a moment she didn't speak. Then she smiled.

"Maybe not," she said.

"What is it, Evie?"

Evie turned to the picture again. "Flea didn't do it," she said. "Now I know the answer. Come on!"

She stood and picked up her bike.

"Now I have the real proof!"

Guilty!

They jumped on their bikes and pedaled back out of town. Back down Carter's Mill Road. Past the Lewises', past Mrs. Hansen's house. They didn't stop until they reached Matt's house. Matt was in the driveway dragging the trap into the garage.

"Stop!" said Evie.

"What do you mean?" said Matt. "Are you ready for the meeting?"

"There's not going to be a meeting," said Evie. "It wasn't Flea."

Matt frowned. "You have the proof in your hand."

"Yes," said Evie. "I have the proof. The real proof. The proof that Flea is *not* guilty."

She held up the picture.

"Look."

Matt and Joe and Megan leaned over the picture.

"I don't see anything but a guilty dog," said Matt. He turned away.

"Wait a minute, Matt," said Joe. "Let's see what she has to say."

Evie pointed to the picture. "Look right there," she said, pointing to the inside of the trash can.

"It's black," said Matt.

"Look again, carefully."

Matt and Joe and Megan looked hard at the picture.

"Look at those," said Evie. Inside the trash can were two small glowing spots of light. Two dull orange spots. Above the spots were three pairs of smaller orange spots.

"What is it?" said Matt.

"Let's see your nature book," Evie said.

Matt pulled the book out of his pocket and handed it to Evie. She flipped through the book and then held it up. At the top of the page it said "Eye Chart."

"Look how Flea's eyes are glowing white. Look at the chart."

The chart had a list of different animals. Beside each animal's name was the color that its eyes glowed in the night.

She pointed to the first line of the chart.

Bright white eyes . . . DOG.

She read from the book. " 'The eyes of certain animals shine when light hits them. Sometimes you can identify an animal by the way its eyes shine.'

"Now look at the trash can again. What do you see?"

"Dull orange spots," said Joe. "Close together."

"There is definitely an animal in the trash can," said Megan.

"What?" said Matt. "What is it?"

Evie ran her finger down the chart.

Yellowish-white eyes . . . BOBCAT.

Bright yellow eyes, close together . . . RACCOON.

Bright white eyes, in a tree . . . PORCUPINE.

Dull orange eyes, close together . . . POSSUM.

Matt's mouth dropped open. "A possum?"

"It must be," said Evie.

"A possum!" Matt said again. "But what about the little spots?"

Evie looked at Megan and smiled.

"Babies!" they said together.

"It could be," said Joe. He sounded interested. "There are a lot of possums in these woods. They do carry their babies on their backs. But they don't usually come up to the houses unless they're hungry."

"She's hungry," said Evie.

Joe frowned. "A hungry animal is a problem."

"We've got to help them," said Evie. "Wild animals don't belong in neighborhoods."

"That's what my dad said," said Matt. "He got permission from the Nature Center to use this trap. If we can capture the possums, my dad will help us take them into the forest and release them."

Megan and Evie looked at the trap, then up at Matt.

Matt grinned. "Looks like you need us in your club after all."

"Couldn't we just borrow that trap?" Evie asked.

Matt shook his head. "No way," he said. "Make us members."

Evie signaled to Megan. They walked to the edge of the yard and whispered. Then they walked back.

"Okay, here's the deal. We make you members . . ."

"Yeaaay!" Matt and Joe yelled a victory yell.

Evie held up her hand. "Wait, I didn't finish. We make you *honorary* members for this case. Then if it works out, if there are no pranks and no problems, we make you members. Agreed?"

"Agreed," said Matt.

"Let's do it," said Joe.

Evie, Megan, Matt, and Joe pulled the trap into the backyard. Matt opened the door of the trap and propped it with a stick.

"We need some bait," said Evie. "What do they eat?"

"I don't know," Matt said, opening the nature book. "Let's look it up. Fruit, nuts, berries . . ."

"That's good," said Evie. "What else?"

"Grubs, insects, crayfish, and dead animals," he continued.

"Yuck!"

Evie decided on some grapes and a peanut-butter cracker.

Megan and Joe raked the soil around the trash cans until it was smooth.

They stood back and looked at their work.

"Tomorrow we'll know for sure," said Matt.

"Yes," said Evie. "Tomorrow we will know."

"We'll meet at seven o'clock sharp."

Early the next morning the girls and Flea ran back to Matt's house.

The soil was covered with prints—small star-shaped prints, about two inches long.

Matt looked at his book. "Possum prints!" he said.

Flea began to growl. His hair stood on end. He danced around the trap and yipped.

"We caught something!" Joe yelled.

They ran to the trap and looked inside.

A small gray animal lay quiet and still on the trap floor. It had a white pointed face and a long pink tail. Peeking over its back were three small babies. Their black button eyes stared at the children.

Evie stepped closer to the trap. "Is she dead?"

"Stay back," said Joe. "She's not dead. She's just pretending to be dead so we'll go away."

"She's 'playing possum,' " said Matt. "But do stay back. I promised my dad that we wouldn't touch the trap if it caught something. Remember she's wild and she can bite. Look at this." He held the book out to Joe.

" 'Possums have fifty sharp teeth, more than any mammal in America,' " Joe read out loud.

Evie and Megan stepped back.

"It also says a possum can grin!"

"Hey, girl," Evie said in a soothing voice. She knelt down and leaned forward but did not go any closer

to the cage. The possum didn't move. The babies didn't move.

"She's not grinning now," said Megan. "She looks so pitiful!"

Matt and Joe knelt beside the girls.

"Hey, little guys," said Matt to the possums in a voice that Evie had never heard before. "We're going to help you."

"Poor babies," said Megan.

"Poor mama," said Evie.

"Poor trash-can robber," said Joe. "Hey, I have the perfect name for her."

They all looked at Joe.

"Guilty!" he said.

Case Closed

A wooden box with wire on the side bounced in the back of Mr. Morrison's van. Inside, the possum lay still and quiet. Beside the trap was a large picnic basket.

Evie, Megan, Matt, and Joe sat in the seats of the van and watched the forest go by.

Mr. Morrison drove. As they rode through the forest he told them about the trap and what he had learned from the Nature Center.

"Wild animals are a problem not just in our area," he said, "but all over the country. As cities grow we're taking over their territory. It's a problem for us and for them."

"Why for us?" Evie asked.

"Because wild animals like raccoons and foxes and skunks can spread rabies."

"What about possums?" Evie glanced back at the trap.

"They don't usually get rabies. That doesn't mean they couldn't. It's just not common for possums. That's why the Nature Center gave me permission to release Guilty and her babies in the forest."

Evie looked out the window and watched the trees. They needed a good place for Guilty. She knew the forest would be better for her than the neighborhood. But how would they know when they found the right place?

Mr. Morrison continued. "I knew it was some kind of wild animal. These boys thought it was a dog."

"I know," said Evie.

Matt cleared his throat. "I'm sorry we accused Flea, Evie," he said.

Evie smiled. "That's okay," she said. "I admit it did look like he did it."

Evie looked over at Megan. Megan nodded.

"Megan and I have come to a decision," Evie said.

Matt and Joe looked away from the window to Evie.

"We have decided to let you two be members of the Pet Patrol." She waited to hear them cheer, but there was silence.

Matt cleared his throat again. "I don't know how to tell you this," he said. "But . . . well . . ."

"We're starting our own club," said Joe. "An animal detective club. We are at your service anytime."

Evie smiled. "You guys *are* good detectives." She thought back to the way they had made the track pit. For just a second she was sorry that they weren't in the club.

The van bumped on the mountain roads.

"Now that we've solved the mystery of the trash cans," said Megan, "I hope we can find a good home for Guilty and her family."

"Then we can eat!" said Joe.

They drove a little farther. They watched more trees go by.

"How about here?" asked Matt's father. He pulled over to the shoulder of the road. He turned off the van and looked at the kids.

"Check it out," he said. "I'll wait for your verdict."

Evie, Megan, Matt, and Joe got out. They looked down the small hill. Below was a stream. Surrounding the stream were trees and bushes.

"Evie and Megan?" said Joe. "You know a lot about animals. What do you think?"

"Let's investigate," said Evie, "like good animal detectives. Come on."

They hiked down the hill to the stream and looked around. They looked up and down the stream.

"There's plenty of water," said Evie.

"And there are probably crayfish in the stream," Megan added.

Joe and Matt checked out the trees and bushes. "There are nuts for them to eat," said Matt.

"And blackberries, too," said Joe.

"I think this place is perfect," said Matt.

"I want to be sure," said Evie.

She walked along the stream some more. Then she stopped and called the others.

"Yes," she said, "this is the place. Look!"

The other kids gathered around Evie. They looked down at the ground where Evie was looking and smiled.

This was it.

In the soft sand beside the stream was a small footprint. A small star-shaped print, two inches long.

"Bring the box, Dad!" Matt called.

Matt's father brought down the box. He put it beside the stream. He attached a long cord to the latch.

"Wait," said Joe. He motioned for everyone to get

back. "We have to be careful when we release them. Possums look gentle but they are wild things."

Evie smiled. "Wild things *are* dangerous, but they're not all bad," she said. "Sometimes they're just misunderstood."

They stood back from the box. Evie pulled the cord. The latch on the door popped open. The mother possum pushed the door wide and sniffed the air. The three babies held tightly to her back as she inched out of the cage. She sniffed again and scurried toward the brush at the edge of the stream. Sniffing and running. Sniffing and running.

"Case closed," said Evie as she watched Guilty run.

"Case closed," agreed Megan.

"Case closed," said Matt.

"Case closed," echoed Joe.

The mother possum reached the edge of the brush and stopped. She turned one last time to look at the children. Then she pulled her face back in what looked a lot like a possum grin and hurried into the woods.